Lydia Dabcovich

SLEEPY BEAR

E. P. DUTTON NEW YORK

for Emilie McLeod
who understands bears

Library of Congress Cataloging in Publication Data
Dabcovich, Lydia.   Sleepy bear.
A Unicorn book.
[1. Bears—Fiction.   2. Hibernation—Fiction]   I. Title.
PZ7.D12Sl   1981   [E]   81-9729
ISBN 0-525-39465-6   AACR2

Published in the United States by
Dutton Children's Books,
a division of Penguin Books USA Inc.
375 Hudson Street
New York, New York 10014
Editor: Emilie McLeod   Designer: Riki Levinson
Printed in Hong Kong by South China Printing Co.
10 9 8 7 6

IT'S GETTING COLD.

LEAVES ARE FALLING.

BIRDS ARE LEAVING

AND BEAR IS SLEEPY.

HE FINDS A CAVE.

IT SNOWS

AND SNOWS.

BUT BEAR IS COZY
IN HIS CAVE.

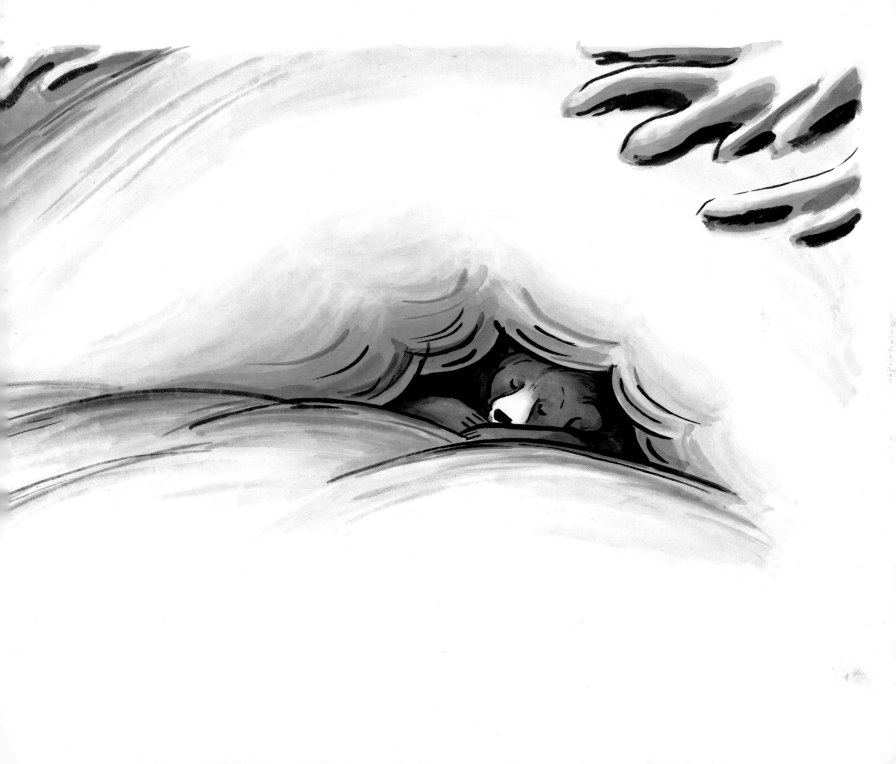

THE SUN COMES OUT AGAIN.

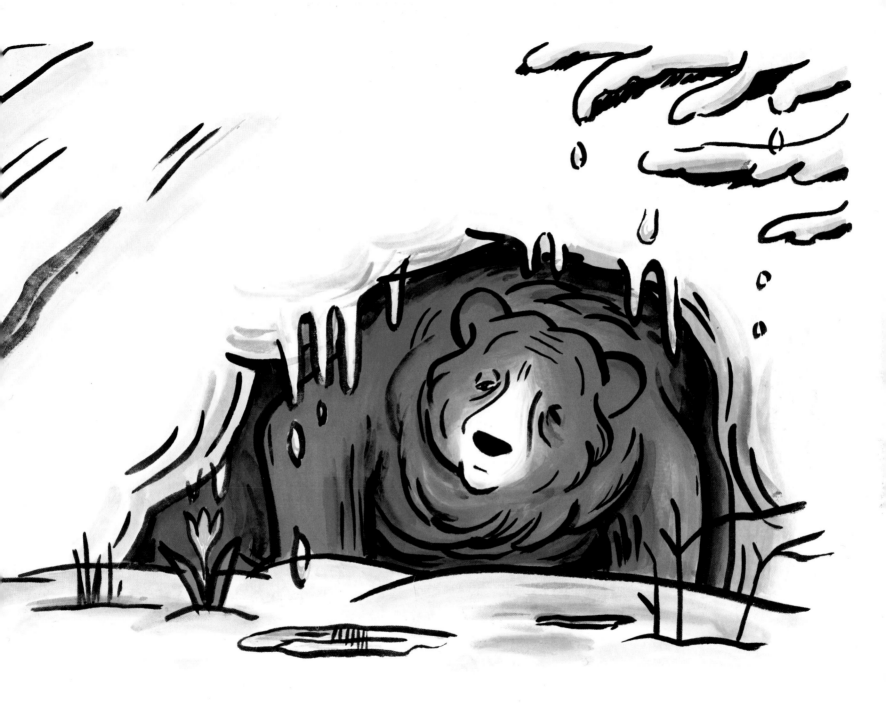

BIRDS COME BACK.

BUGS COME BACK.

BEES COME BACK.

BEAR REMEMBERS HONEY.
HE FOLLOWS THE BEES.